FORBIDDEN LOVE:
EYE OF THE STORM

LENNY HARVEY

FORBIDDEN LOVE:
Eye of the Storm

ISBN: 9798854814973

My grandfather, Oliver, a true Romany Gypsy, told me this story years ago. I have filled in the gaps and dramatized the story for your enjoyment.
The story begins with the search by a young gypsy to unravel a 150-year-old murder mystery, Love, war and the supernatural. The final ending is based on a true story.

Oliver Scarrott Brinkley Smith 1922
A true Romany Gypsy

Table of Contents

Kizia Harvey, Scarrott Brinkley
& son Lenny Harvey

Kizia and Lenny Harvey, Scarrott, Brinkley
Belvedere marshes 1944

1944 Belvedere Marshes.

About the Author

Greetings! I'm an octogenarian with a loving family – two children and seven adorable grandchildren. In my prime, I stood tall at six feet and weighed a sturdy 225 pounds, but time has, alas, caused me to shrink a tad.

I do grapple with dyslexia and didn't have the privilege of a formal education. Nevertheless, my family's encouragement has inspired me to share some captivating tales about the vibrant Gypsy culture, preserving them in our family archives.

My heart swells with pride for my Gypsy heritage, passed down by my remarkable mother, Kizia Scarrott Brinkley Harvey. She was not only a stunning Gypsy lady but also an unwavering animal lover.

My upbringing adhered to the strict Romany principles instilled by my grandparents, who were true Romany gypsies. Raised mainly by my grandparents, uncles, and aunts, I formed a sibling-like bond with Vera, my mother's younger sister, who was six years my senior.

Our childhood was a nomadic adventure, hopping between various locales like St. Mary's Road and different Gypsy camps. We worked at hop picking, fruit picking, flower hawking, rug crafting, totting, and logging.

My life was a constant shuffle, living in rented rooms with my mother and her boyfriend, and occasionally residing with various family members. Consequently, I went to over a dozen schools.

If you're curious, my father was overseas, fighting in Europe during the war, and it wasn't until I turned fifty that fate brought us together. But that's a tale for another day.

During my early years, I took on various family trades, all while evading school. I dabbled in selling flowers, heather, logs, and tar blocks, and even found myself working as a bookie's runner.

My journey in these endeavor's is chronicled in my book, "Romany Gypsies," available on Amazon.

At the tender age of fourteen, I conveniently passed for sixteen, which opened doors to employment on ships undergoing repairs in Greenhithe, along the Thames estuary. By the time I truly turned sixteen, I underwent training on the merchant navy's training vessel, the Vindicatrix, eventually earning my stripes as a seaman. This maritime journey continued on and off until I was around eighteen.

My eclectic career spanned nearly seventy years, encompassing roles as a scrap metal merchant, ship breaker, dance hall promoter, and a licensed firearms holder. I served as a contractor to the Ministry of Defense, entrusted with security clearance to access MOD dockyards and facilities.

My adventures extended beyond British shores, taking me to Eastern Europe, including Russia, Ukraine, and Crimea. During one memorable trip, I advised the Crimean Navy on disposing of the former Russian Black Sea Fleet anchored in Sevastopol. Moreover, I played a pivotal role in organizing HRH Prince Charles' visit to Sevastopol. As a security adviser to the Ukrainian government,

I accompanied the royal security detail and had the honor of being presented to HRH, who is now King Charles III, of course.

In the 1990s, I was contacted by the Crimean Ministry of Health to provide pharmaceutical products. Unfortunately, this venture eventually resulted in my financial downfall. I've experienced both wealth and destitution multiple times in my life.

There are many more chapters in my life's story, but those tales will have to wait for another day. In the meantime, I'd like to mention my three books: "Romany Gypsies," a self-biography of my youth; "The Devil's Gypsies," a gripping Gypsy tale, albeit fiction; and "FORBIDDEN LOVE: Eye of the Storm," a supernatural thriller also in the realm of fiction. You can find them all on Amazon.

Behind the scenes of these literary ventures stands my wonderful wife, Lynne, my steadfast companion of fifty-eight years. Her sensible guidance and support have been instrumental, even though, at times, she felt it was like trying to halt a runaway train. She mostly succeeded, though I must admit that I didn't always heed her advice, and the wheels occasionally came off.

Stay safe and entertained,
Lenny Harvey.

CHAPTER ONE

The Dawkins Family

1745

The wealthy Richard Dawkins family had been land own-ers and farmers for generations. Richard Dawkins and his wife Martha in her early forties, had two beautiful twin daughters Priscilla and Lillian aged sixteen and a son named Henry aged fourteen.

The Dawkins family resided in an opulent manor, the cen-terpiece of their extensive estate. Their wealth flowed from a combination of farming and a prosperous horse breeding operation.

This manor occupied an elevated plot of land, adorned with meticulously manicured gardens that gracefully guided visitors to its imposing entrance. Within its walls, opulence reigned supreme, and the Dawkins family lived a life of unbri-dled luxury.

The great hall of the manor played host to regular soirées, attracting the local gentry, who arrived resplendent in their fin-est attire. Horse-drawn carriages rolled into the rear carriage yard, where dedicated staff attended to the graceful vehicles and their majestic steeds. Guests, accompanied by the staff, were then ushered through the splendid front gardens to the manor's majestic entrance.

The Manor

Richard Dawkins 1745

Martha Dawkins 1745

Priscilla Dawkins 1745

Lillian Dawkins 1745

Henry Dawkins 1745

Richard Dawkins allowed a large family of Romany gypsies, the Brinkley's, to camp beside the river that ran through his land. For generations, the Brinkley family has camped and worked on the Dawkins Farm and nearby farms. They earn their living through fruit picking, hop picking, and general labor, relying on the fairness and goodwill of the farmers to survive.

There were strict rules surrounding gypsies - it was forbidden to associate, fraternize or form a friendship with gypsies, under some circumstances, it could mean deportation or a death sentence. Of course, this did not apply to the getry farmers who used the gypsies as cheap labor. Oliver Brinkley's son, Thomas Brinkley, was a good-looking and talented young man who was skilled in horse riding and the overall management and control of horses. He was only seventeen years old, but was called upon regularly to work at the farm stables, harnessing and saddling horses for the farm and the Dawkins' family. His father Oliver, a fearsome bare Knuckle Champion and an expert with horses and riding had passed these skills onto his son.

Thomas mother Patience was a woman in her late forties, still beautiful for her age.

Patience Brinkley 1745

Romany camp beside the River. 1745

Richard Dawkins brought his twin daughters a pair of horses, black and tan three-year-old hunters. Despite Pike's objections, as he was the stables' headman, Mr. Hawkins instructed Oliver and Thomas to school the horses for his daughters. Elijah Pike, who managed the farm and stable, felt offended by what he saw as an insult against his leadership as the head stableman. He had a dislike for gypsies, particularly Oliver and Thomas, who he envied for their expertise and familiarity with horses. Pike continuously looked for an excuse to berate Oliver and Thomas. On one occasion, he told them that he did not want them to bring their satchel bags with them; he claimed things had gone missing from the stables, and he did not want them stealing things and hiding them in their bags.

Thomas Brinkley 1745

Oliver Brinkley Sr 1745

The next morning, as Oliver and Thomas arrived at the stables to start work, Pike confronted them - they were to give him their satchel bags. Oliver handed them over, and Pike hung them on a hook outside the stables tack room. Oliver and Thomas were busy training the two horses when, at midday, Oliver requested their food satchels from Pike. However, Pike rudely refused, telling them to wait until they finished their work at around seven in the evening. Oliver explained politely that they needed the food to continue working for the rest of the day, but Pike flew into a rage and lashed out with the short whip he carried for whipping the stable boys, catching Thomas across the face.

Oliver was on him in an instant, gripping his wrist that held the whip. "If you move another effing muscle I'll grind your fat face into the ground," he whispered quietly in Pike's ear "Do you understand me?". Pike trembled with fear, he knew the reputation of Oliver as a bare-knuckle fighter in the Gypsy community, and he could feel the strength of Oliver through his grip on his wrist. He dropped the whip.

"You ever raise your hands to another of mine, I'll drown you in the river." Oliver said, "Do we understand each other?"

Pike grunted, rubbing his wrist.

George Smith v Oliver Brinkley 1725

"Come on Thomas we have work to do." Oliver walked away. Thomas looked at Pike with a burning hatred, nodding at him, as if to say my turn would come.

Over the next few months, Oliver and Thomas broke and schooled the horses, making them suitable for the sisters to ride side-saddle as was the custom. Priscilla and Lillian came to the stables every day to see the progress of the horses, questioning Oliver and Thomas as to the condition and improvement of their horses.

Oliver and Thomas thought that the horses were now ready to be ridden. Oliver suggested to Richard Dawkins, the girl's father, that they should start to ride the horses.

Pike was not pleased.

CHAPTER TWO

Lillian & Thomas

The girls' father employed Mr. Popping and his wife to instruct the sisters how to ride; they were considered experts in etiquette for young ladies riding side-saddle, and this was considered essential to protect a woman's virginity, as Mr. and Mrs. Dawkins wished for their daughters to marry into the landowner gentry it was of the greatest importance they remained virgins.

Mr. Popping and his wife were a distinguished-looking couple, both in their early sixties and dressed in expensive riding clothes. Mr. Popping was dressed in a black wool military styled double-buttoned frock coat, a fawn and gold woven waistcoat with a white shirt and a high-standing collar along with white moleskin breeches that were buttoned at the knee. He had on his riding boots and accessorized with a black top hat, gloves, and a riding crop.

Mr. Popping

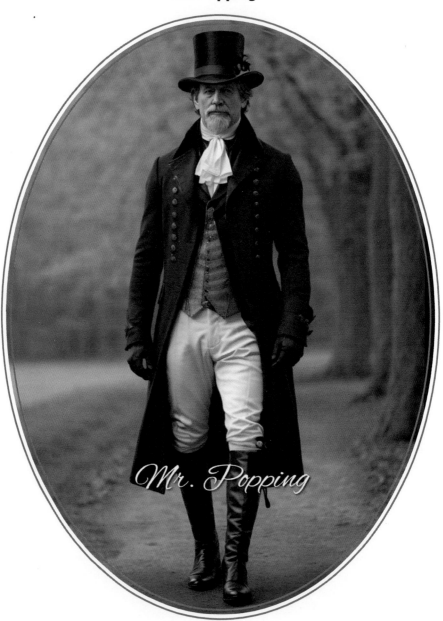

Mrs. Popping a distinguished looking woman in her sixties dressed in a white high collar shirt with a long black riding habit with military styled buttons and a waistcoat. Accessories included a gold double fob chain a wide curved-brimmed top hat and riding boots.

Mrs. Popping

Mrs. Popping
1745

Oliver and Thomas were skilled at preparing the horses for the young ladies and ensuring their safety during the ride, whether on foot or horseback.

Priscilla and Lillian were stunningly beautiful. They arrived at the stables early for their first lesson, dressed in long black riding habits, specially designed for riding side-saddle, with flat, broad-brimmed silk hats with low crowns tied on with ribbons. That morning, Mrs. Popping demonstrated how to sit on the saddle, with the left foot in the stirrup and the right knee over the pommel on the front of the saddle, giving a more secure grip.

While she was doing this, Mr. Popping instructed Oliver and Thomas on how to help the women onto the horses.

"Oliver, Thomas, please pay attention," Mr. Popping said "A woman needs two men to mount a horse side-saddle. One has to hold the horse's head still and the other to help the woman to get on the horse."

Although Oliver and Thomas had been doing this for years, they stood politely and listened to the side-saddle and etiquette instructor. "One man should stand in front of the horse, holding him still by the bridle. The woman then grips the saddle pommel with her right hand and her left hand on the right shoulder of the person that is to lift her, he will do this by bending and clasping their hands and fingers together," he demonstrated.

Mrs. Popping, looking directly at the sisters, continued "The lady will then put her left foot in the groom's clasped hands, bending her knee, with the help of the groom and a slight lift she will be lifted onto the saddle, where she puts her right knee over the pommel, like this," she demonstrated.

Mr. Popping then continued, "A woman also needs a man to help her get off the horse, taking her foot out of the stirrup, and giving her left hand to her attendant." When he beckoned Thomas forward, Mrs. Popping demonstrated dismounting. "The lady is dependent on a groom when dismounting and could not travel or hunt without help beforehand and after, do you all understand," said Mr. Popping.

Both horses were saddled ready for riding. "Let's take the horses out to the meadow and start our lessons on mounting and unmounting before we actually start to ride," Mr. Popping said. "Miss Priscilla, would you like to be first?"

"Yes," Priscilla said as she stepped forward with a laugh, "I can't wait."

Oliver guided a horse towards them, and Thomas stood ready for Priscilla to place her left foot in his clasped hands. He lifted her up and she effortlessly mounted the saddle, indicating her prior experience. "Thank you, Thomas," Priscilla said, looking pleased with herself.

Mrs. Popping looked on approvingly. "Come on Lillian, she called out, it's your turn let's go out for a ride." Lillian stepped forward. Oliver led her horse over to her, and Thomas clasped his fingers together. Lillian put her foot into his hands, and with a slight spring, she jumped into the saddle; Thomas thought she had slightly paused as she put her foot into his hands, long enough that for him to smell her fragrance. She was lovely, and just as confident as Priscilla. Thomas looked up at her. "Thank you,.

Thomas." she said, with a smile, again slightly longer than necessary

Priscilla Dawkins

Priscilla Dawkins
1745

Lillian Dawkins

Every morning, Mr. Popping would lead the riding lessons at ten. As Lillian practiced riding side-saddle, she found herself increasingly drawn to Thomas for his easy-going nature and handsome appearance. After a few days, as they rode through a meadow, Lillian said she was tired and wished to sit down on a nearby fallen log and rest.

Priscilla told Thomas to stay with Lillian. "We'll meet up on the way back," she said.

"Yes, Miss Priscilla," Thomas replied. He then helped Lillian to dismount, and she sat on the log.

Thomas walked a short distance away and sat down on his haunches, keeping an eye on Lillian. After a while, Lillian asked Thomas to come and sit next to her. Thomas hesitantly walked over and sat at the end of the log. "Thomas, I'm not going to bite you," Lillian said, laughing "I just want to ask you about your family and the things that interest you, besides horses of course, she laughed.

Lillian and Thomas found that they were very similar in their attitude to life and their love for animals. After that day, Lillian took every chance available to talk to Thomas; they began meeting secretly walking through the forest hand in hand, and soon enough they were deeply in love. This didn't go unnoticed by Elijah Pike—he reported back to Mr. Dawkins that he thought Thomas was becoming too familiar with Miss Lillian.

Elijah Pike, the farm and stables manager, was responsible for the horses. This included selecting their feeds, ensuring their health, and grooming them. Pike, who had worked at the stables since he was a boy, Pike was a tall man standing over six feet and was around forty years old with gray hair a big black moustache with a piercing stare.

He lived in a nearby small, farm cottage with his wife and four children—three boys aged five to ten and a girl who was around twelve. The entire family worked on the farm, and although Pike was a skilled horseman and performed well in his job, he had a tendency to be a bully, a secret drunkard, and a womanizer.

The stable lads were terrified of him. He would beat them with his whip at every opportunity.

The young female farm workers were also very wary of him, as he had the reputation of assaulting girls in the stables and threatening to have their families thrown off the farm if they did not let him have his way with them.

Elijah Pike. 1745

Following Pike's false and malicious reports about Lillian and Thomas, Mr. Dawkins forbade Lillian from seeing Thomas. Additionally, he told Pike that the Gypsies were no longer permitted to work at the stables.

Pike watched Lillian closely, hoping to catch her meeting with Thomas. Lillian pretended to go for a ride alone, and Pike assisted her in saddling her horse and getting on. She rode off towards the river.

Thomas Horse and Cart bye the River

Pike secretly followed her on foot, ensuring that he remained hidden. Lillian eventually arrived at the river, where Thomas was waiting with his horse and cart. Thomas assisted Lillian in dismounting, and they hugged each other.

Pike crept up behind them using the cart as cover. He sprang from behind the cart with a wooden club in his hand and struck Thomas on the head knocking him unconscious.

"You killed him!" Lillian screamed.

Pike grinned. "Now it's your turn, Miss Lillian."

He struck Lillian on the side of the head with the club, knocking her to the ground. He then stripped her and looked down at her—he would ravish her and, of course, blame it on Thomas.

Thomas shook his head to clear the haze from the blow, and when picked himself up from the ground, he saw the terrible scene—his beloved laying naked on the ground with Pike standing over her. He leapt at Pike, knocking his club out of his hand, and they both tumbled off in a life-and-death struggle. Pike, being the stronger man, rolled on top of Thomas and began to strangle him.

When she recovered from her unconscious nightmare, Lillian stood up and quickly took in what had happened. She picked up Pike's club from where he had dropped it and brought it down on the large man's head in blind fury. His grip on Thomas weakened, and Lillian hit him again. Blood spurted from his head in a fountain, and Pike fell sideways off Thomas, dead.

Lillian bent down beside Thomas, he opened his eyes and gasped. "Are you alright?"

"Yes, my love," she whispered, "and Pike is dead. I killed him with his club."

Thomas went to the cart and took out some clothes. "Put these on," he said.

As she quickly got dressed, Thomas spoke, "If he's found, they will surely hang me for his murder."

"No," said Lillian, "it was me that killed him. I'll tell my father."

"Who do you think they will want to hang?" Thomas asked, "it won't be you."

"What are we going to do, Thomas?" Lillian asked.

"Let's throw the bastard in the weir," Thomas replied, "he should soon be washed out to sea."

Together, they dragged Pike's lifeless body to the edge of the weir, where he was unceremoniously rolled into the river. As Pike floated face down towards the weir's edge, an eerie moment transpired; something caught on Pike's clothes, flipping him over just before he went over the weir. His lifeless body then caught on the weir's edge, momentarily suspended with one arm raised high above his head; fist clenched in what seemed like a last gesture of hate. As he plunged into the swirling waters below, Pike let out a loud deep growl as the air was expelled from his lungs

The couple stood in shock, witnessing a scene that seemed straight out of hell. With Pike gone, they knew they had to move quickly to avoid detection. "We better get on our way," Thomas said.

"I love you," Lillian replied, "let's go."

Together, they decided to continue their journey, embracing an uncertain future hand in hand. Their love had overcome darkness, and they were determined to face whatever challenges lay ahead.

Elijah Pike Evil till the End

Elijah Pike, fist clenched as he plunged into the swirling waters below.

CHAPTER THREE

The Brinkley family 1910

Oliver's parents, Walter and Patience, came from generations of Romany gypsies going back hundreds of years. They had roamed the British countryside all their lives, the wagon pulled by Paint, their big black and white cob. As Paint got too old to pull the wagon, he retired to graze and wander the marsh or wherever they laid up with the other horses.

The Brinkley Wagon

Romany wagon Interior 1900s.

Bowtop wagon

Bowtop interior

Walter Brinkley a handsome slightly graying big man, he was a fearsome bare-Knuckle fighter, he dressed gypsy style; a big horseshoe gold ring on his finger, line shirt, and a and black choker neck scarf, waistcoat with gold fob chain, brass buckle belt, dark trouser, with black boots and a trilby hat.

(See photo Oliver and Tiny)

Walter Brinkley Sr 1900

Patience a pretty woman, had brown eyes. She wore her wavy gray hair long and dressed in a traditional gypsy's long dress and tough brown boots. Her jewelry included silver and gold beads chain around her neck, long earrings, rings on her fingers and bracelets on her wrists. She was skilled in the traditional Romany way of life and taught her daughters the skills; from flower making, to peg making from the hedgerows, cooking, cleaning and how to look after the animals. Walter and Patience brought up to this hard life, in a world full of prejudices and the build-up to the first world war.

Patience Brinkley. 1910

Walter Brinkley jr 1910

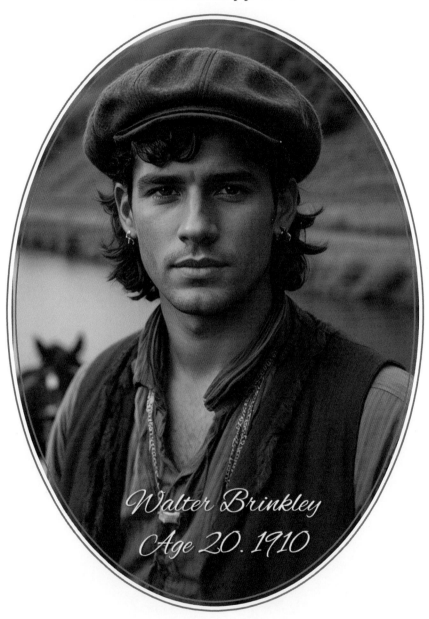

Rhoda Brinkley age 18. 1910

Oliver Brinkley age 17. 1910

Oliver Brinkley
age 17, 1913

Wally Brinkley age 15 1910

Wally Brinkley
Age 15 1910

Ocean Brinkley age 12. 1910

Frenni Brinkley age 10. 1910

Gentile Brinkley age 8 1910

Walter looked like his father—handsome, with brown eyes and long dark hair. He was of slight build and nearly six feet. He often rolled the sleeves of his collarless shirts, and always carried his red choker neck scarf, and a flat cap on his head. Walter worked on the farms independently and would soon be leaving the family to find his way in life. Sixteen-year-old Oliver was a handsome young man. He and Wally had his family's brown eyes, dark hair, and wiry build. At ten, Frenni was a good horse rider, learning from his brothers. He was tall for his age and dressed as his brothers, although his handed-down clothes didn't quite fit as well.

Rhoda, the eldest sister, was of marrying age, and skilled in the traditional Romany way of life. A beautiful girl, she always dressed like her mother in traditional gypsy-style long dresses, gold chains, long earrings, rings and bracelets. Walter and his wife kept an eye out for a suitable husband for her. Six years younger than Rhoda, Ocean was a petite and pretty girl who already had a keen resemblance to her mother and sisters. She and eight-year-old Gentile, dressed like her mother and older sister, though each sister liked to add something to Gentile's dress, making her more doll-like with flowers in her hair.

Oliver and his siblings never went to school, so they never learnt to read or write. School wasn't much use in their world, but they were all extremely intelligent, skillful and thoughtful of others, and loved and cared for all their animals. They all could be relied on in any situation.

The Three Sisters

The family's skewbald Gypsy cobs, known as the three sisters, with their feathered legs and golden long manes, were all bought from the marsh horse sales for their color and temperament as yearlings. Over the years, they were schooled to pull the wagons, and they were dearly loved as part of the family.

Blossom, the biggest and oldest, earned her name because she was chosen when the cherry blossoms bloomed. She pulled the big Vardo. Gorgeous, named by Rhoda as soon as she saw her as a yearling, pulled the Bowtop wagon. Little Rosie got her name because she was chosen when the little wild roses bloomed in the English hedgerows.

The Brinkley family possessed two wagons and a cart. The big square-top Vardo was pulled by Blossom, the Bowtop by Gorgeous, and the cart by Little Rosie. Paint, their big piebald cob, was now semi-retired. Two young brown and white cobs, Flower and Heather, both named after the marsh's flower sprays, were tethered to the back of the cart. They also had a big black lurcher dog named Tiny who walked up and down the wagons, guarding the family. When traveling, he liked to sit on the cart, and when laid up, he lived under the big wagon or in the bender tent when it was too wet or cold.

Oliver had three sisters and three brothers. Walter, Rhoda, and Wally were twenty, eighteen, and fifteen. Ocean was twelve, Frenni was ten, and Gentile, the youngest, was eight.

Flower & Heather

It was a hard life. When traveling, the family walked beside the wagons and cart, with the youngest sitting on the back of the cart with Tiny, keeping an eye on the horses. Walter usually walked beside Blossom, and Oliver walked beside Gorgeous. The girls took turns sitting on the front wagon box, holding the reins.

The girls slept in the Bowtop wagon on a bed under the main bed. There was side-upholstered seating that could also be used as a bed. The women kept the wagons in pristine condition, polishing and cleaning the small ornate windows in the cabinets and the larger windows around the wagons. The china in the cabinets was for display purposes only, never used. The eating plates and tools were kept in the pan box on the back of the wagons.

Walter and Patience lived in the big-wheeled square-top wagon, painted red with gold scribed inlays. It had a porch at the front with an ornate glass double half door and outdoor coach lamps. The wagon had been passed down through the generations and was dearly loved and cared for, just like their horses. The wagon stove warmed the wagon in the winter; all the cooking was done on the outside fire. The ornate glass and brass oil lamps were magnificent. The interior was upholstered in red and green fabric with ornately embroidered cushions. Some nights were magical, with the oil lamps burning inside and carriage lamps outside. The wagon gave off an ethereal red and gold glow, and the outside fire threw the reflection of its flames on the ornate glass windows and half-covered glass door.

Oliver and his brothers erected a large bender shelter using long branches, which they covered with a thick blanket and oil tarp. They kept their harnesses, ropes, and equipment in the bender, and all the brothers slept inside it, except during the coldest winter nights when they slept in the wagon.

Tiny would guard the equipment in the bender. Their beds were made from a layer of branches to keep them off the ground and cotton paillasse stuffed with leaves, reeds, or straw, with multicolour patchwork blankets made by the girls. When it was too wet to work outside, they worked in the bender, making pegs from the hedgerows. The boys loved the marsh and being close to their horses; they could hunt rabbits for food while their sisters collected heather and plants to make lucky sprays and the tranquillity of the marsh. The family was always ready to move on at a moment's notice when forced to by the authorities. They earned their living in the traditional Gypsy way—farm labouring, fruit and hop picking. The girls sold pegs, flowers, and heather sprays, and the men and boys sold logs, broke horses in for farmers and the gentry, and traded in horses.

Bender Shelter Tent

Walter Brinkley & Tiny the family Dog

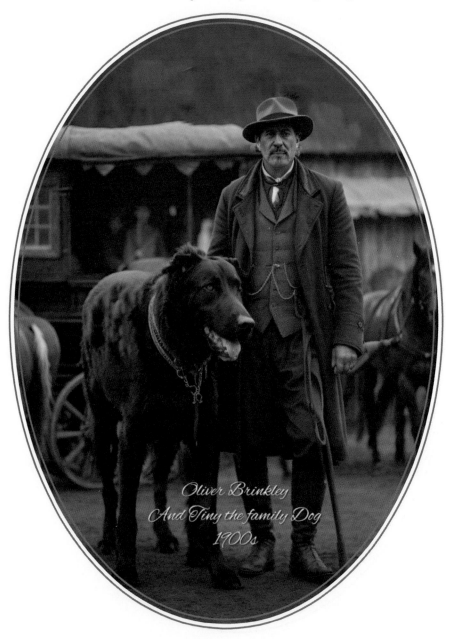

Oliver Brinkley
And Tiny the family Dog
1900s

Priscilla 1910

Oliver was a talented horse rider, learning to ride horses on the marshes for as long as he could remember. That day he had walked down to the lake on his own checking on his father's horses. He lay on the coarse grass beside the marsh lake watching the horses standing in the water drinking. It was a beautiful day, so peaceful and tranquil. As he lay there content and happy, he drifted off to sleep, he thought he could hear a girl's voice.

"Good morning, Oliver. How are you today?" He opened his eyes, there was no one there, the horses hadn't been disturbed.

He thought he must have been dreaming, he closed his eyes, and then he heard a laugh.

"Keep dreaming Oliver, you will hear me more clearly." He opened his eyes again, but no one was there. He leant on one elbow and took in the horses and lake.

Yes, he smiled, *I definitely have been dreaming.* Oliver closed his eyes again.

After a few minutes, the soothing girl's voice called to him again "Keep your eyes closed Oliver. You will learn that the more you smile and are happy, the better you will hear me." Oliver smiled to himself. He was dreaming. The voice clearer this time, said, "I've been watching you with the horses; that's when you're most happy and content. It makes me feel happy too."

"Yer, I love them," Oliver said, "I'm going to have lots of them when I'm older and get a few quid."

Oliver opened his eyes. *Who had I been talking to?* he thought. He laughed out loud.

This time the girl's voice said, "I'm glad you are happy Oliver, it's easier to talk to you once you've accepted that I'm real."

"No, you're not," laughed Oliver, "it's a dream."

"Are you awake now?" the voice asked.

Oliver jumped up and looked around. "Yes, I am," he said, laughing to himself.

"Sit down, Oliver," the voice urged, "you'll frighten the horses."

"No, I won't."

"Oh, come on, sit down. We can talk if you want." Oliver sat down.

"I know this is hard to understand, Oliver, but please listen; I need your help and want to be friends. I am real."

"No, you're not," said Oliver, laughing. *This is a dream.*

Look around you Oliver, you are awake, this is not a dream.

Oliver looked around; the horses were standing in the water, ducks 'were quacking, and there were all the usual sounds of the marsh.

He frowned and shook his head.

"I told you, you're not asleep,"'

"What do you want?" Oliver asked, startling himself, and quickly looking around as if someone would hear him and think him strange.

"Just to be friends," the voice answered. "Please sit down, and I'll try to explain."

Oliver sat down on the grass. *What am I doing listening to an invisible person's voice? h*e thought, smiling to himself.

"Oliver, my name is Priscilla. I'm sixteen years old and used to live in a big manor house near the wheat fields."

"What, the one that's a ruin?"

The old Manor House

Manor in Ruins
1910

"Yes!" the voice replied, "that's been a ruin for a hundred and fifty years. My dad said no one even remembered when people lived there."

"Your father's right, nobody has been living there for nearly a hundred and fifty years."

Oliver couldn't believe he was having this conversation with an invisible person. He was confused, so he jumped up and walked back to the wagon. He was restless for a day or so, even letting one of his brothers check on the horses.

With a mother's tuition, Oliver's mother asked him what was troubling him. "Your mind is not on your work."

"Nothing, mother," Oliver replied.

« Have you met someone, his mother smiled.

"No mother. No," he replied. She smiled again.

After a couple of days, he returned to the lake to check on the horses. All seemed calm, he smiled to himself, "I knew it was all a bloody dream," he said out loud.

The horses all looked up, startled and then a voice said, "Now you've frightened the horses."

Oliver's mouth dropped open.

"Shut your mouth, Oliver, before you swallow a fly." Priscilla laughed.

Oliver, sat down on the grass, bewildered,

"I'm sorry if I've confused you, Oliver," Priscilla said, "I know how difficult this must be for you, as it is for me, you know."

That's a woman's logic, thought Oliver.

"All right, what do you want?"

"I told you; I want us to be friends."

Oliver shook his head, "That's going to be a bit hard if I can't even see you, ain't it?"

"Alright," Priscilla said, "you don't have to shout, I can hear you."

Am I actually having a row with someone I can't even see? Oliver thought.

"I'm sorry," Priscilla added, "I'm so frustrated at you not being able to see me yet."

"What do you mean, yet?"

Priscilla laughed. "You will be able to see me soon. It takes a little time."

"How much time?" asked Oliver.

"The more we talk, the sooner you will see me; I don't know why, that's just how it is."

"Alright," Oliver said, "are you a ghost?"

"No, I'm not," Priscilla replied indignantly.

"What are you then?"

"I'm a lost soul," she said.

"How do you know?" Oliver asked.

"Well, I don't remember dying; you have to die to be a ghost, don't you?"

"I don't know," Oliver rubbed his chin, "I've never met a ghost, only you, and you're just a voice."

"I'm not just a voice," Priscilla retorted, "I'm a real person, and you will soon see."

Oliver met with Priscilla whenever he was alone, and this went on for a couple of weeks.

CHAPTER FOUR

The Storm

O n a fine summer's day, Oliver was sitting by the marsh lake, talking to Priscilla, when suddenly, his' eyes widened. "I can see you," he said.

"Can you?" she said, excitedly.

Priscilla was sitting beside him on the grass. She leaned over and kissed Oliver's cheek. He couldn't feel her lips, but his heart missed a beat. It was as if she was in a mist, and the mist gradually cleared.

Priscilla was beautiful. Dressed in a white lace-covered long dress, with little summer flowers embroidered around the neck and sleeves. She had big blue eyes, ivory colored skin, and her golden hair glistened in the sun, like a vision from heaven.

Oliver gasped. He had never seen anyone so beautiful. "You-," he stammered, "You are beautiful."

"Am I?" Priscilla gasped. "Oh Oliver, do you think so?" she cried.

Oliver met Priscilla every chance he had. She told him about her life; she had lived with her father, mother, brother aged fourteen and twin sister aged sixteen at the farmhouse, in the year 1745. That summer, the weather had been exceptionally hot, for weeks, with exceptionally violent storms, thunder and lightning, and little rain. The earth had started to crack and shrink.

Her entire family was in the wheat fields. Her father was supervising the field hands as they cut the wheat. Her mother and brother were coordinating the house servants to arrange tables with food and water for everyone during the midday break.

The day began with clear skies, but as midday approached, dark blue clouds suddenly appeared. The clouds grew darker and lightning and thunder followed, but no rain fell. They felt a strange sensation coming from the ground, causing their skin to tingle and their hair to stand on end. The sky exploded and lightning crashed to the ground. A thunderous roar came from the sky, with a whirlwind that pulled them all up into the clouds.

The next thing Priscilla remembered was floating in the clouds with lightning flashing all around her. She could hear her mother, father and brother calling for her, but she couldn't find them. Then the voices faded away, and she was alone.

Priscilla Eye of the Storm

"I drifted through endless time and space, always returning to Earth," she said "Once, when I returned to Earth, there was a huge lightning storm, near the wheat fields. I heard my family calling for me again, but the storm died away, and so did the voices."

"These storms come only once in every generation," she told Oliver, "and the storm is due this summer. I need help to enter the storm to rejoin my family. It does not matter where that may be, but we would all be together."

Oliver listened quietly. "How do you know all this?" he asked.

"There are other lost souls, lost in indifferent ways and time," Priscilla said, "they all have a little piece of knowledge of how to return, I've learnt a bit, I just have to try. To return to your loved ones, every lost soul must have an earthly family or true love. I have neither," Priscilla cried.

"What can I do?" Oliver asked.

"Oliver, from our time together, I know we would have loved each other if we had met in a different time and place," Priscilla said quietly, "that's why I had chosen you to see me."

"Do you feel the same about me?"

"You already have said that Priscilla, you know the answer."

They clasped hands, and though they didn't physically sense the touch, the profound love in their hearts was palpable. They made sure to spend as much time as possible in each other's company, riding over the marsh on Paint, the large black and white cob. Paint adored Oliver's presence and could feel the affection Priscilla had for him. Oliver often brought Paint treats of bread, which would cause him to whinny, neigh, and snort with delight. Paint could sense Priscilla's presence as she whispered in his ear, and he could hear her every word.

Oliver would place a rope head collar on Paint, then mount him and Priscilla would appear behind him. They would ride across the marsh, and sometimes simply walk with Paint, conversing about their lives and listening to the marsh's sounds. They shared stories and made plans like lovers do, despite knowing it could never be.

Priscilla told Oliver that she had a twin sister, her name was Lillian, she had disappeared the year before the storm and was never found. "What happened to her?" Oliver inquired.

Lillian was a beautiful girl, identical to Priscilla in every way; she had met a gypsy boy named Thomas Brinkley from a nearby gypsy camp on her family land, and they had fallen in love. Lillian's father, Richard Dawkins did not approve of the gypsy boy and forbade Lillian from seeing him. They believed Lillian had intentions of running away with the boy.

Lillian Dawkins 1745

Richard had let them camp with their three wagons, four carts and half a dozen horses every winter, doing odd jobs on his farm before moving on in the summer to other farms where they worked as farm laborer's, picking crops.

Their father was outraged at the loss of his daughter, and he went to the gypsy camp to see the boy's father, Oliver Brinkley. Oliver told Richard he didn't know where they had gone, only that when Lillian had visited them, he could see that they were in love.

Oliver had told them that it would be difficult for them, as he knew Richard would not approve of their relationship.

Thomas had taken his own horse and cart, with all his belongings and left a few days ago; boys of his age were taught to care of themselves, so it was not unusual for them to seek a life of their own. Richard told Oliver unless his daughter was returned to their home, he would not allow Oliver's family to stay on his land and would inform the surrounding farms not to employ him or his family.

Oliver said he would try to locate the runaways. The same day, a search party found Thomas' horse and cart with all their belongings by the river near the weir; Lillian's horse was tied to the cart, It was thought that they had gone swimming near the weir, got into difficulties and their bodies washed down the river and out to sea, never to be found.

Thomas' father confirmed that he would not leave his horse and cart unattended. They must have drowned. Both families were devastated by the loss of their beloved ones.

Oliver took his son's horse and cart back to his camp, and Thomas's cart was burned in a ritual as is the Romany custom for the dead. Lillian's family held a church service to commemorate her short life.

Oliver's family was made to move on from the farm; the surrounding farms would not employ him or his family, just as Richard Dawkins had threatened, for he did not want the gypsies on his land any more. He blamed them for the tragedy.

Oliver had observed an old wooden bucket submerged in the earth, containing water, conveniently accessible to the horse. Nobody else seemed to have noticed it.

It is thought the Brinkley's travelled on around the Kent hop fields and camped in the winter on the Belvedere marshes.

As for Pike, he was never found.

"That's a sad story," Oliver said.

"Yes," Priscilla replied, "we never got over losing Lillian, but I never believed Lillian and Thomas died on the river."

"What do you believe happened then?"

Priscilla thought for a minute, "Is it true that Romany Gypsies burn the wagon or carts of the departed?"

"Yes, that's true."

"I just don't know," Priscilla said, "I never felt that she had died."

"I'm sorry," said Oliver.

"Do you know Belvedere Marshes?" Priscilla asked.

"Yes, I know them well. We have camped there many times," Oliver nodded.

"Can we go there?"

"What for?" Oliver answered.

"I just have this feeling that's where they went."

"You said they had no horse or cart or belongings?" Oliver asked.

"I know, but they could have walked."

"Yes," said Oliver, "but they would have to stay with someone when they got to the marshes."

"I understand the Brinkley's were a large family that travelled all over the country for over a hundred and fifty years."

"Yes," Oliver nodded, "any family member would give sanctuary to another and keep any secrets. It has been a hundred years since your sister went missing; there would be no trace on the marsh, even if they were there at some time."

"Oliver, please take me there, I need you to show me the gypsy ways."

"I would have to tell my family where I was going and why," Oliver said. "what could I say?"

"I know this is difficult for you Oliver, but I cannot do this without you, please help me."

Oliver, told his parents that he needed to go away for a few days to settle his mind on his future. He asked his father if he could take Paint; he said he would ride him along the river path, buying hay for paint from the watermen, and a parcel of food that his mother made him up for a few days.

Before departing, he inquired of his father, "Dad, where are the graves of our family located on the marsh?"

His father gave him a puzzled glance before responding, "Some are buried on the elevated land near the trees, while many others are buried alongside the rivers, highways, and layups. I've shown you over a hundred years."

"I know, Dad, it's just good to remember."

Oliver slung an old saddle and halter on Paint, tied the sack of food, and rolled some rope, a coat and a blanket in oilskin. He left early the next morning, riding on Paint along the river, till he felt the presence of Priscilla.

Priscilla and Thomas. 1910

"Thank you, Oliver." She had appeared behind him on Paint.

They travelled on till early afternoon then stopped at the river bank where Paint could drink. As Paint grazed on the thick grass along the river drinking from the shallows, Oliver ate his lunch of bread and cheese.

Priscilla sat beside Oliver. "This is wonderful, Oliver," she said, "how long will it take to get there?"

"I thought you knew everything?" he turned to Priscilla.

"No, Oliver. I don't. I'm a lost soul, I only know certain things; I don't understand it myself, so please be patient with me," she laughed.

"OK," said Oliver, "we should be on the marshes tomorrow, midday."

That night, Oliver set up camp under some trees near the river, took the saddle off Paint, and tied the horse to the tree.

He sat next to Priscilla. "What are we going to be looking for when we reach the marsh?" he asked.

"I think you already know," Priscilla replied, "we'll look for graves, or any talk of Thomas and Lillian from people still living on the marsh."

Oliver nodded. "I thought that. I'm going to get some sleep now."

He pulled his blanket up and quickly fell asleep.

Oliver woke up just as it was getting bright. He quickly cleared up the campsite, making sure Paint had enough water, and embarked on his journey towards the marsh. As he went along, he weaved through passing barges and made room for the massive shire horses pulling them.

Around mid-afternoon, they reached the marshes. There were dozens of Vardos laid up there, with bender shelters and tents, horses grazed on the open marsh, barking dogs and kids shouting and running around.

"Oliver, this is wonderful," Priscilla whispered, "I've never seen anything like it. Where does your family stay?"

Oliver laughed. "My family is all there," he pointed, "but my aunt Rhoda's wagon is over on the other side; she's my dad's sister, and his other sister Kizia lives in another camp."

Oliver rode through the camp to waves and greetings. "Oliver where's the rest of them? Where's your dad?"

Aunt Rhoda, a gray haired woman in her late sixties, her husband, Arthur had died a few years ago, she now lived on her own, with her song birds and dog, her old Vardo had seen better days. As Oliver and Paint made their way up to the wagon, his aunt sat on the porch front feeding songbirds from a bowl . Their dog, a big lurcher growled, then as if recognizing a family member, wagged his tail in greeting.

Aunt Rhoda

CHAPTER FIVE

Belvedere Marshes

liver saw Aunt Rhoda, who was sitting on the steps of her wagon, dispensing songbird feed from a bowl, just as she did every morning. "Hello, Aunt Rhoda," called out Oliver. She turned around, her face illuminated with delight upon seeing Oliver atop Paint.

"Why, young Oliver and Paint!" she exclaimed. "Get down and let me have a good look at you." Oliver dismounted Paint and warmly embraced Aunt Rhoda. She affectionately patted Paint and planted a kiss on his forehead.

"To what do we owe the pleasure?" she inquired, her curiosity piqued. "And where is the rest of the family?"

"They're all back in the marsh down the river," replied Oliver. "I just needed a brief respite," he confessed.

Come on said aunt Rhoda, I'll make you a nice cup of tea and something to eat. "It's been a bit lonely since your uncle Albert died. It's lovely to see you. If you're staying for a while you can stay in the Bender here."

"Thanks, Aunt Rhoda, perhaps for a night or two."

Romany Gypsy Family on the Marsh

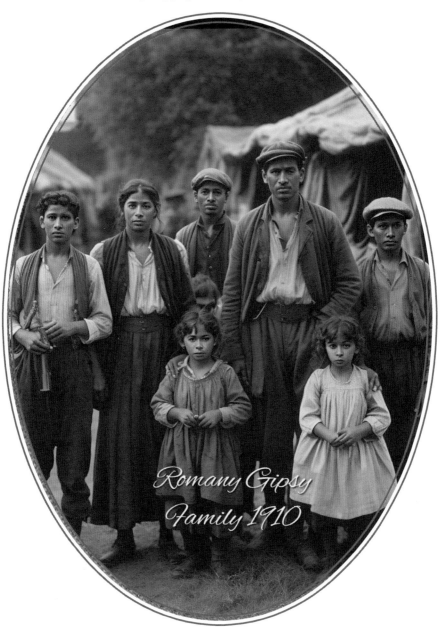

Romany Gipsy Family 1910

After hanging a net of hay from the back of the wagon with a big bucket of water for Paint, Oliver sat down on a chair in front of the camp fire with his tea and a big bowl of rabbit stew and bread. He stretched back on the chair. "Thank you, Aunt Rhoda. I needed that."

"Good," Aunt Rhoda said, ", now tell me about all that's happening with the family."

After a few hours of exchanging gossip and family stories, Oliver got up. "I better see Paint, and walk him across for a bit of grazing."

"Go on," Aunt Rhoda said, "I'll clear up, and we can have a talk when you come back, but only if you want to."

Oliver walked Paint out onto the open grassland, and after a while, Priscilla appeared beside him. "You all right, Oliver?" she asked.

"It's a bit' unsettling when you just appear and disappear," Oliver spoke up.

"I'm sorry, but I told you I don't fully understand why this happens. I only know I appear when I feel you want to talk to me." said Priscilla.

"You're sure nobody else can hear you or see you?"

"Yes, Oliver," Priscilla replied, "only you and Paint can sense me."

Oliver told her his aunt knew there was something wrong. "What am I going to tell her?"

"Perhaps she may know something about your family going back a few generations," Priscilla replied, "you can ask if she has heard of anyone called Thomas or Lillian."

Oliver and Priscilla walked whilst Paint happily grazed on the marsh grass.

"How long has your family camped on this marsh?" she asked

"Gypsies have been here for hundreds of years, my family for generations," Oliver answered, "I'll talk to Aunt Rhoda this evening."

That evening, after more rabbit stew and tea, Oliver and his aunt sat around the campfire. The lurcher sat beside Rhoda, taking in the warmth. "Can you remember any family or talk years and years ago of Thomas or Lillian who ran away to be together on the marsh?"

Rhoda thought for a while. "You know Oliver I do remember my mother Genti, talking about a gypsy boy who ran away with a gorger girl, but that's nothing new is it?" she laughed. "'It's either a son or daughter that runs away with a gorger." She looked up at Oliver. "Is that what's troubling you, Oliver? A pretty gorger girl?" she smiled.

"No, no," Oliver chuckled, "it's not that. I'm trying to help a friend."

"How can we help your friend?" Aunt Rhoda asked with a smile.

"Well, my friend is trying to trace a family going back a hundred years or more."

"What are the names your friend is looking for?" asked Aunt Rhoda.

"Brinkley," Oliver offered "Thomas and Lillian."

"Well, we better go and see your grandmother Genti and see if she knows anything," Aunt Rhoda replied, "we'll go tomorrow."

"How did it go?" Priscilla asked Oliver as he made sure Paint had water and hay.

"You didn't make me jump this time," Oliver replied, "I must be getting used to you appearing out of the blue. Well, Aunt Rhoda didn't know anything, but she wants me to go and see my grandmother in the morning; grandmother Genti is over ninety years old. Let's hope she can remember anything."

After seeing to Paint and turning him out to graze the next morning, Oliver and Rhoda walked a short distance to his great-grandmother's wagon. This Vardo was even more beautiful than Rhoda's, with bright red and gold, and ornate glass doors. Grandmother Genti sat on the wagon porch listening to her songbirds and smoking her pipe.

Rhoda waved. "Good morning, gran. Look who I brought to see you." She pushed Oliver forward.

Granny Genti

"Hello, gran," Oliver said.

"I can't see you properly my boy, but I would know that voice anywhere. Come up here and give your old gran a kiss, Oliver."

Oliver climbed up the steps and gave gran a kiss. She held his hand and a tear ran down her cheek. "So good to see you, Oliver. Rhoda make the tea," Grandmother Genti said, "Oliver's got to tell me all about the family."

Oliver sat down on the wagon steps and told Gran all the latest news till Rhoda said she would tell Grandmother Genti more the next day. "Gran, Oliver is trying to help a friend find some information on a family member a few generations ago. I thought you might remember something."

Gran laughed. "Oliver, you be careful of them gorger girls— don't matter how pretty they are, the Gypsy life is too hard for them."

Before, Oliver could answer, Gran went on "What's the name you're interested in?"

"Well Gran," Rhoda said, "there's our Brinkleys, Thomas and Lillian, going back a hundred years or more."

Gran took a puff of her Pipe in deep thought, after a while she spoke, "There are' plenty Thomases and a few Lillians. My grandfather ran away with a gorger girl, or so the story goes."

"You know Oliver, there are some secrets best left alone," Rhoda said.

"Gran, do you know where they went?" Oliver said.

"Sorry, Oliver. I can't say."

Oliver thanked Grandmother Genti.

The next day, Oliver walked Paint to the high ground where the trees stood as he talked to Priscilla about what to do next. Among the trees, there were several memorial stones indicating family graves. A few yards away, there was a cluster of flowers on the ground. Oliver gazed at the stones, but they were too weathered to make out any names.

The Resting Place

"Can you read any of them?" Priscilla asked .

"No," Oliver replied.

A little girl's voice came from behind him. "Are you praying to your mum?"

Oliver turned around, and faced a pretty little girl with blue eyes and blond hair, aged about six.

Oliver smiled, "Err, no," he squatted, "just thinking out loud."

"Are you visiting someone here?" Oliver asked.

"Oh no," she replied, "no one here. Do you live here?" "Yes," said the girl.

"My name's Oliver Brinkley."

"I know. We all saw you ride in." the girl replied, "my sister is seventeen. She said you were very handsome and she would like to marry you.

Oliver laughed out loud, and the little girl looked disappointed. "You're not already married, are you?"

"No," Oliver replied, "I'm not."

"That's good. Our wagon's next to your gran's. You should come and have a cup of tea with my dad, then you could ask him if you could marry my sister, Lily. Her real name is Lillian." Oliver looked at her "Her name is Lillian?"

The girl nodded. "Pretty name, isn't it? My dad said it's a bit gorger, but Mum wanted it."

Priscilla whispered in his ear, "tell her you'll come for a cup of tea with her dad."

"I'll pop in for a cupper with your dad," Oliver said.

"Can you come this afternoon?" The girl asked with an excited smile.

"Say yes," Priscilla nudged him.

"Yes." said Oliver.

"That's kushti. I'll go and tell my dad and sister. See you this afternoon." The little girl left Oliver alone.

"Ask her what her name is," Priscilla said.

"What's your name?!" Oliver called out to the girl.

"Priscilla!" she shouted over her shoulder as she skipped off, "but you can call me Prissy!"

"Her name is *"Priscilla?!"* Priscilla exclaimed.

Prissy Smith

Oliver nodded and said, "that's what she said. She lives in the next wagon next to my Gran's, and neither Gran nor Aunt Rhoda ever said a word about it."

As they walked back to Aunt Rhoda's wagon, Priscilla expressed her shock at hearing Lillian's and my names. "Why would they choose those names if they were not somehow related to the family?" she asked.

"Who knows," Oliver replied.

"It sounds like you have made a big impression on the local gypsy girls," Priscilla said, laughing.

In the wagon, Oliver told Aunt Rhoda what had happened on the high ground with the little girl.

Rhoda explained that she recognized the name Lily from the Smiths' family's daughter but forgot it was actually Lillian.

"Of course." Oliver could not explain the significance of Priscilla, so he had never mentioned it.

Rhoda suggested she pop along to the Smith's wagon, and talk to the parents, explaining that Oliver was just being polite with the little girl, and was not looking for a wife.

"Yes, that would be good," Oliver replied, "but I would still like to meet them."

When Rhoda came back from the Smith's wagon, she told him they understood and apologized for little Prissy's boldness. "You are welcome for a cup of tea, Oliver. I will go with you."

When they called on the Smiths later that afternoon, Grandmother Genti was also there, sitting on a chair by the fire. William Smith, aged about thirty-five, was a tall graying man with a welcoming smile and warm nature. In her early thirties, his wife Catherine was beautiful and petite, with fair hair and the biggest blue eyes you ever saw.

William Smith

Their daughter, Lillian, was as pretty as her mother with a shy, engaging smile. Prissy the little girl, couldn't wait to introduce Oliver to her older sister, Oliver and Lily, now aware of the matchmaking skills of little Prissy, politely said hello to each other.

Formalities over, they all sat around the fire, drinking tea. William Smith knew Oliver's father from various wagon layups and family connections. This is how gypsies socialized and kept up-to-date on family affairs; they exchanged family updates and gossip, laughed and enjoyed each other's company. It was hard to keep news from travelling amongst gypsies.

Eventually, William spoke "I've been talking to your gran here," he said, nodding towards Grandmother Genti as she smoked her pipe, "she told me you've been asking about the names.

Lillian Catherine & Prissy Smith 1910

Thomas and Lillian. I suppose you are wondering who we named Lillian after; your family and mine are connected, you are entitled to know."

Lillian Smith

Lillian Smith
Age 17 1910

Catherine gave her beautiful smile, and said, "Oliver, my great-grandmother was Catherine Smith, and my great-grand-father was Elijah Smith. I don't know where they were born, only that they were married at a young age here on the marsh, in the old gypsy way, jumping over a broomstick."

Catherine and Elijah lived in a wagon on the marsh all their wedded lives. They had four children, two girls and two boys. They both died aged about sixty-five; Elijah from tuberculosis and Catherine from a broken heart. Their wagon was burnt on the marsh, and they were buried together on the high ground. "I looked but couldn't make out the inscriptions on the marker stones," Oliver said.

"That is because they are buried a short distance away from the trees," Catherine replied.

"I did notice flowers growing out of the shadow of the trees and a bunch of flowers laying there," Oliver remarked.

"That's where they are buried—there is a stone marking their resting place."

Oliver looked at little Prissy, "I thought you said you had no one resting there,"

Prissy smiled and laughed out loud, "They're under the trees, where I placed the flowers before you arrived." She laughed again, clearly pleased at her little deception.

"What about the children?" asked Oliver.

"The two boys and one of the girls travelled on their own way," Catherine said, "the other girl, my grandmother, stayed on the marsh and married Levi Smith. They had six children; four boys and two girls. My mother was one of the girls, Catherine, and she married Jacob Scarrott. I have four brothers and three sisters. My dear husband here, William is also a Smith from another part of the country. We have two daughters and a son Albert, who is travelling with family at present."

Oliver let out a deep breath. "That's some family we have here." Grandmother Genti and Rhoda both nodded. Lillian smiled at Oliver and William patted him on the back, not finished yet,

"Catherine's the one that can read in the family, and she's got something to show us all."

Catherine got up. "I won't be a minute." She climbed the wagon steps into the wagon, and after a few minutes, she returned, holding a wooden box. She sat down with the box on her knees.

"Oliver, I have a letter from my great-grandmother," Catherine said, "would you like me to read it for you?"

Oliver sensed Priscilla gasp and exhale, then she whispered in his ear, "Oliver, I should not be listening to this. I'm not your family."

Oliver gritted his teeth, and under his breath said, "yes you are; you are Lillian's sister. Stay here.

Catherine, frowned and looking at Oliver. "You alright, Oliver?"

Oliver nodded. "Just felt cold for the moment." He felt Priscilla take a deep breath. "Please read the letter, Catherine."

Catherine took the letter from the box. It was old and brown - decades before it had been tied with string and a candle wax seal holding it together. Now, the wax had dried and cracked.

She held the letter up for everyone to see, then read aloud:

Catherine Smith 1910

Catherine started to read the Letter

Private
Priscilla Dawkins.
The Manor Farmhouse in the County of Hertfordshire.

Oliver felt Priscilla gasp and stifle a sob, and he only just kept himself composed. Little Prissy had now fallen asleep on Lillian's lap.

"I have not read this letter before," Catherine said, "as the wax has cracked off leaving the letter unfolded, with only the thin string holding it together. Perhaps this is the time to read it."

Catherine pulled the old string off and straightened the old parchment paper out. Inside was the letter, also sealed with wax. Now cracked and fragile, the wax easily came off and with a sigh, Catherine started to read.

Private
Priscilla Dawkins.
The Manor Farmhouse in the County of Hertfordshire.
My beloved Sister Priscilla,
Please forgive me for deceiving you. I did not drown, neither did Thomas. We are alive and well.
We had to make it appear that way, to stop father from finding us. Father would surely in his anger have inflicted terrible revenge on Thomas for taking me away from the family. Nothing could be further from the truth - I love Thomas very much. We arranged our subterfuge by the river with the help of persons I shall not name at this time, in case this letter falls into father's hands.
We have enough money to start our new life together. This money, chattels and love have helped us build our new lives.

Furthermore, we are now married and are very happy. We have changed our names, so Father can never find us. I don't know how I will get this letter to you, but I will try.

Once again, please forgive me.

Your loving sister

Lillian.

THE LETTER

Private
Priscilla Dawkins.
The Manor Farmhouse in the County of Hertfordshire.

My beloved Sister Priscilla,
  Please forgive me for deceiving you. I did not drown,
neither Did Thomas. We are alive and well.
We had to make it appear that way, to stop father from finding us.
Father would surely in his anger have inflicted terrible revenge on
Thomas for taking me away from the family. Nothing could be further
from the truth - I love Thomas very much. We arranged our subterfuge
by the river with the help of persons I shall not name at this time, in
case this letter falls into father's hands.
We have enough money to start our new life together. This money,
chattels and love have helped us build our new lives.
Furthermore, we are now married and are very happy. We have
changed our names, so Father can never find us. I don't know how I
will get this letter to you, but I will try.
Once again, please forgive me.
Your loving sister
Lillian.

Everyone stayed silent, and then Oliver said, "that's where the name Priscilla came from. The address on the letter."

"Yes, lovely name, isn't it?" Catherine asked.

"Yes," Oliver smiled at little Prissy, who was still asleep.

Priscilla was whispering in Oliver's ear, "she was alive all the time. I knew, I knew she was alive. I told you so, didn't I Oliver," Priscilla cried.

It was all Oliver could do to keep from shouting. *Yes, she was alive this whole time.*

Grandmother Genti

puffed on her little clay pipe, nodding and smiling. Catherine said to her, Your knew all the time didn't you, gran?"

Grandmother Genti nodded. "Yes, my dear, but only through word of mouth, handed down in the the family. I and others were sworn to secrecy."

CHAPTER SIX

The Resting Place

Everyone listened intently as Grandmother Genti explained that she knew of the letter, but it could not be delivered to Lillian's sister.

"You have to remember that in the time this letter was written, most gypsies could not read or write—there was a great prejudice and hostility towards gypsies, dating back to the days of slavery, and the hanging of gypsies just for existing. Everywhere, gypsies were sought after. Gypsies aged fourteen or over, or those found in the company of gypsies, were put to death."

Everyone gasped, while Grandmother Genti paused for a short while as if composing herself. She took a breath, and slowly let it out. "Children were taken into service. The others were ordered to leave the realm or face death. In later years, many were shipped off to the colonies as slaves. Things are not much better now, but you must remember, farmers are the gypsies' lifeblood, working on the farms, crop picking and the like. Without them, it would be even harder to survive.

"If a farmer goes against a family of gypsies for whatever reason, as you all know, they would have to keep travelling till they found a farm that would employ them. If the word spread from farm to farm amongst the farmers not to employ certain gypsies it would mean added hardship.

So, anything that would give rise to such things was closely guarded, such as running off with the farmer's daughter.

Everyone let out a breath in agreement. Grandmother Genti paused again, sucking on her old clay pipe and slowly nodding her head in deep thought. Everyone waited for her to continue. After a while, she let out a small cloud of smoke and continued,

"Thomas and Lillian changed their names and lived on the marsh, earning their living in traditional ways. Lillian soon became adept in the Romany way of life. They were now known as Catherine and Elijah Smith and lived their lives as such. Had children and are now at peace on the high ground.

That's the story of Elijah and Catherine Smith.

It's still best to be untold, for prejudice and hostility follow us everywhere.

Oliver let out a deep breath. "Phew, Gran, that's some story."

Everyone nodded. "Everyone understands," said Catherine. "Yes," they all nodded.

"That story gives us all something to think on," William said, "we should have a prayer at the resting place, perhaps tomorrow."

"Yes," everyone agreed on having it after breakfast on the high ground. "Time for bed now," Rhoda said, "let's call it a day. We'll take Gran in our cart tomorrow. Goodnight everyone."

Oliver and Rhoda returned to her wagon, and while Oliver watered and fed Paint, Priscilla appeared beside him. "Thank you, Oliver. I know that was very hard for you, listening to the letter being read out with me whispering and crying in your head."

"Yes it was, but do you feel better now you know what happened to your sister?" said Oliver, "oh, yes," Priscilla replied "I always thought that Lillian would let me know if she was alive. I now know why she couldn't, but she did try. I'm looking forward to visiting their resting place tomorrow."

The High Ground

In the morning, Rhoda asked Oliver if he could put Paint in her old cart, so they didn't have to walk up to the high ground. Oliver, harnessed Paint to the old cart, and they set off up the hill to the high ground. Paint made easy work of pulling the little cart with Oliver and Rhoda.

Grandmother Genti stood with the Smiths on the high ground, with a faint wisp of smoke coming from the pipe in her mouth. Oliver pulled Paint up beside them and exchanged greetings.

"Right, let's go over the resting place," William said as he walked carefully through the carpet of flowers to a memorial stone laying flat in the ground. They all followed William, Granny holding onto Rhoda's arm with one arm, and the other holding her walking stick,

Looking down at the Inscription, Oliver could just make out,

In Loving Memory of
Elijah and Catherine Smith.
Rest in Peace.
1795.

Underneath the inscription, there was some Romany, unintelligible script.

"There is always a gypsy stone Mason on the camp to carry out stone inscriptions," William said. They all stood in silence as Catherine read a prayer from her bible, and they chorused an "Amen".

They all stood for a while, taking in the tranquility and beauty of the high ground, as the river snaked through the down on the Gypsie camp.

"OK," said William, "let's go back for a cupper, and say goodbye to Oliver."

CHAPTER SEVEN

Under the Stone

"I think I'll just stay for a while. I'll see you back at the wagon," Oliver said.

"I'll go back with gran, see you later Oliver," Rhoda said.

"Oliver can walk me to the cart?" Grandmother Genti asked. Rhoda started down the path back to the carts, and Oliver and Grandmother Genti stayed. Later, as they walked to the cart, Grandmother Genti asked Oliver, "Could you read the script at the end?"

Oliver replied, "No, Gran, I couldn't make it out."

Grandmother Genti stopped and held onto his arm, taking the pipe out of her mouth. She whispered, "It says,

"Ava tuke phenel te chavó ando shavoripe tume so prala."

Elijah and Catherine Smith

After kissing him on the cheek, she put the pipe back in her mouth and said, "Right, get me up into the cart. See you for a cup of tea later."

As Oliver walked back to the resting place, Priscilla appeared beside him. "It was a lovely thing for you all to do at this resting place," she said.

"Yes," Oliver nodded, "it seemed the right thing to do. Everyone was at peace."

"I could see that," Priscilla replied, "I loved hearing that letter read; I felt Lillian was close. Do you think this is really their resting place?"

"Of course," Oliver stopped, "Don't you?"

"It just seems strange not to see Lillian and Thomas's names on the stone.

"Look down," Oliver said, pointing to the stone, "can you see that Romany script?"

"Yes," Priscilla said, "what does it mean?"

Oliver quietly said,

"Beneath you will find the peace you so wish"

I don't understand said Priscilla in frustration.

Oliver bent down and ran his fingers around the stone. He then took his folding knife out of his pocket and bent down again.

"What are you doing?" Priscilla asked as he ran the blade around the stone.

Oliver kept running his knife around the stone, and when he could not dig any deeper, he tried to raise the stone up. It would not budge. "Oliver, what are you doing?" Priscilla asked.

"Just wait." Oliver continued to dig and pry at the stone. Suddenly the stone moved up a fraction. Oliver got a better grip on the stone and lifted it up.

The stone was resting on a bigger stone. Oliver moved the inscription stone to one side and laid it on the ground. He brushed the dust and soil off the stone, and there was an inscription on the stone.

Inscription

In Loving Memory of
Thomas Brinkley & Lillian Dawkins
Rest in Peace
1795
"Tu les mange ando rodipe tiro so kamav"
"Here is the peace you so wished "

Priscilla let out a scream, of my God, it's really Thomas and Priscilla.

After carefully putting the stone back on top and making sure the earth was trodden back,

Oliver left and went for tea again with the Smiths. After a brief farewell, he called on his granny. "I'm off back home, Gran," he said.

Grandmother Genti looked at his soiled trouser knees and bruised fingers. "Did you find the peace you were looking for?" she asked.

Oliver gave her a big kiss on the cheek, "Thank you, Gran. I did."

Grandmother Genti took the pipe out of her mouth. "Now it is your secret as well, Oliver. Keep it safe."

Oliver nodded, "I will, Gran."

Oliver prepared Paint ready for the journey back. He thanked his Aunt Rhoda, and started the long ride home.

Oliver and Priscilla 1910

CHAPTER EIGHT

In the Eye of the Storm

While Priscilla and Thomas waited for the coming storm, they sat on the bank of the marsh lake, knowing that their time together was coming to an end. Priscilla was happy now. Her life may have been cut short by the storm, but she now knew her sister had had a full and happy life.

The sky started to cloud over, and the wind picked up. Priscilla walked over to Paint who was grazing nearby. The old horse stopped grazing and started to walk towards Priscilla; he knew she was leaving. "Goodbye my lovely boy," she said, "I'll see you again soon." The old horse nuzzled her, and she kissed him and walked back to Oliver.

"It's time Oliver." They held hands and walked to the old wheat field.

As they stood in the middle of the field, the wind started to howl and swirl around them.

The Storm Swirled around them.

"Oliver, you must go now," Priscilla said, with tears in her eyes, "the storm is nearly here."

"What if I stay?" Oliver squeezed her hands.

"You can't, my love, it's not what it is supposed to be. Your destiny is not with mine. We are from different times and places. You know that; there's a great war coming and your country will need you."

Oliver kissed her face, tears in his eyes. He turned and left Priscilla in the arms of the storm.

Above the flashing lightning, wind and the rumble of thunder, he thought he heard her crying and shouting "Father! Mother! Little brother! Lillian!"

All together again. *A lost soul is only lost until it is found.* For the Lord himself shall descend from heaven with a shout, with the voice of the archangel, and with the trump of God: and the dead in Christ shall rise first: Then we which are alive and remain shall be caught up together with them in the clouds, to meet the Lord in the air: and so shall we ever be with the Lord. Wherefore comfort one another. Amen.

Priscilla in the Eye of the Storm

CHAPTER NINE
Paint 1910

Paint 1910

liver's father and older brother were out selling logs on the cart with little Rosy. Their mother was working making flower sprays with Frenni and Gentile. The two gypsy brothers, Oliver and Wally, were checking on the horses, and as they approached, they heard the noise of the horses, whinnying and snorting.

They ran to the marsh lake and saw Paint, their big cob in distress. The black and white cob was slowly sinking in the marsh; he had wandered too far in trying to get a drink in the dry hot summer. He was whining in distress, the horses on the bank stamped their hooves on the dry ground, shaking their heads up and down, snorting and whining back in alarm.

Oliver and Wally usually carried ropes around their necks for making halters for any horses they wanted to take back to the wagon, but the ropes were too short to be of any use.

"You will have to run back to the wagon and get Blossom," Oliver said to Wally, "put her collar and harness on and some long reins, with as much rope as you can find. Make it quick." Wally raced off to get Blossom, while Oliver spread some reeds on the marsh towards Paint. By the time he reached the cob, it was already submerged up to its legs. Oliver stroked Paint gently and assured him that Blossom would soon come to pull him out.

Wally hurried back riding Blossom, with traces ropes and long reins across her neck. The two brothers quickly made up a sling from the ropes, took it out to Paint, and passed it around his haunches. They hurried back to Blossom and hitched the ropes to her collar and harness.

Wally led Blossom by her halter, pulling and urging her on, Oliver was beside Paint, adjusting the ropes and trying to keep Paint calm.

Blossom started to pull Paint free from the marsh, and although he was exhausted, Paint made one final effort to pull himself free. With Blossom pulling, Paint managed to free one leg and he gradually walked out of the marsh.

Oliver soothed Paint as the cob shook on the bank.

Wally took his shirt off, dipped it in the water of the marsh. Then he used the shirt to wash the mud off him with his shirt. Paint gradually calmed down; he lowered his head down to Wally washing his legs and nuzzled him, his long mane hanging over Wally's face.

Paint was born before all the brothers had sisters. When he was younger, he used to pull the big wagon and cart, but he was getting old now; he'd spent these years in retirement on the marsh or wherever they laid up.

Paint and Blossom in the Marsh 1910

One morning, Paint laid down on the grass and wouldn't get up, Oliver and Wally tried to get him up, but it was no good; he couldn't move. The boys stayed with him, stroking his head and neck, comforting him, and reminding him of when he pulled the wagon before Blossom. Taking a few final, labored breaths, he gradually slipped away.

The family would never forget their big black and white Paint Cob. Especially Oliver, Wally Priscilla and Lillian.

Paint

Paint 1910

CHAPTER TEN

The First World War
1914 - 1918

In 1914, Oliver and Wally volunteered for the British army, breaking horses in to pull gun and ammunition carriages. Their elder brother Walter had left and gone on his own way two years earlier; he also volunteered for the army and fought on the western front.

Oliver and his brother Wally were in the same regiment, but due to a change in army regulations after they volunteered, brothers could not serve in the same regiment. They both resigned and rejoined another regiment, Oliver with one name and Wally with another, they were still both together.

Private Oliver Brinkley 1914

Private Oliver Brinkley
1914

Private Wally Brinkley 1914

Private Wally Brinkley
1914

Oliver and Wally fought in the brutal Mesopotamia campaign in what is now Iraq. They fought from the Euphrates and Tigris swamps to the Iraqi deserts. In the last days of the war, the two gipsy brothers; Oliver age, now twenty-two and twenty-year-old Wally, had fought so gallantly for their country, and after four years of fighting in the most appalling conditions, lay badly wounded and dying in the Iraq desert.

War in the Desert

Oliver and Wally Brinkley

Mesopotamia 1917

Oliver and Wally had concussions and multiple shrapnel wounds. But Oliver's kneecap was shattered in addition. They both lay in a crumpled bloody heap, more dead than alive, in excruciating pain, half blind and deaf from the explosions of artillery shells. They were slowly bleeding to death. There was no medical aid coming, most of them were all dead, and there seemed to be no hope.

"Wally! Wally!" Oliver called out as he tried to stand, "We got to get out of here," He jabbed at his brother with his empty rifle, "stop messing about,"

Wally tried to move. "Oh, fuck off. Let me die."

"Come on Wally, help me, I can't stand up," Oliver groaned.

Wally managed to sit up, blood running in his eyes. He wiped away the blood with his sand-covered sleeve and looked at Oliver. "You look like you just fell off your horse and got trampled on," he choked.

"Get me up," Oliver choked, "we've got to get back to our lines. Wherever that is."

Wally crawled over to his brother, "If I can get you up, put your ammunition belt around my neck and your arm through it, then use your rifle as a crutch under your other arm."

Over the sound of machine gun fire and exploding shells, they managed to stand up. "Right," Oliver said, "let's go back the way we came." They staggered a few steps, then fell into a heap on the sand. "

It's no good," said Wally, "we don't have the strength to do it."

"We must," said Oliver, "let's try again." They tried, and again fell back onto the sand. They tried once more, and this time the blast from an exploding shell threw them to the ground. "It's no bloody good," Wally spat. Oliver was choking on the dust swirling around them, "There ain't no help, so get up Wally," he winced in pain.

Then out of the dust and smoke, an image appeared before them. Priscilla and twin sister Lillian, on the back of a big black and white painted cob horse. Paint, whinnying and neighing, stood over them and bent his head down, his mane dangling in their faces.

"Oliver, you must throw something over Paint's neck to hold onto!" Priscilla cried. Oliver, in a daze, painfully threw his empty ammunition belt over Paint's neck. "Grab the other end Wally," he croaked. In a daze, Wally reached up and held the other end of the belt. He looked up and saw Priscilla and Lillian. His eyes widened in his blood-encrusted face. "No need to worry now Oliver, we're already in heaven."

Priscilla Lillian & Paint

"Not yet," said Oliver, "hold onto that bloody belt." With his other hand, he grabbed his rifle. Wally looked around, saw his rifle in the dust and sand and, with one hand, slung it over his shoulder. Paint pulled his head up, lifting the brothers up onto their feet, then he dragged the men along with him, as he walked, just like Blossom and Wally had dragged him out of the marsh many years ago.

Priscilla and Lillian both leaned forward and placed their hands over the brother's hands, holding onto the belt. Strength flowed through them as Paint walked around the bomb and shell craters, never flinching in the face of the rattling machine guns and exploding shells.

"How did you know?" Oliver croaked, "where did you come from?"

Priscilla caressed his mud-stained face "It doesn't matter my love, you both must find the strength to hang on to the belt. You will be safe soon." They staggered along for what seemed like forever, holding onto the ammunition belt that was their lifeline around Paint's neck.

Then as the smoke cleared, they found themselves outside the Army Field Hospital, shaking with pain and fatigue covered in sand, dust and blood. Oliver and Wally looked like they had just emerged from hell; Oliver with one arm through the ammunition belt, and the other draped across Wally's neck and shoulder, was supported by Wally using his rifle as a crutch. Both caked in blood and sand, the whites of their eyes stared out from blackened blood-covered faces. The nurses looked at them in disbelief.

"Get them men on stretchers," the head nurse shouted.

Above the noise of the exploding shells and the shouting nurses, Oliver heard Priscilla's voice, "You will be safe now."

Oliver and Wally spent weeks recovering in the hospital before they were shipped home. Wally recovered. Oliver spent months in hospital, he was later discharged as disabled.

The British defeated the Turkish Sixth Army at the Battle of Shariat in October 1918.

Wally went on to have his own family and children.

Oliver spent the rest of his life in constant pain from his shattered knee. He received a few medals and a meagre war pension for his disability.

He never rode again, nor could get a proper job with his disability, but he did get married to my beautiful, grandmother Alice, who had five children and loads of grandchildren.

Grandad never complained; he just got on with life. He was a real Romany Gypsy hero.

"Grandad" I said, "was Priscilla a dream or real?"

"You know, Lenny," Grandad smiled at me, "life may only be a dream. Enjoy it while you can."

I have a few more stories from my granddad.

Lenny Harvey

THE END

Printed in Great Britain
by Amazon

30441807R00082